The Jumbled Jungle

Brainy Yak, LLC

Let's take a short stroll through a jumbled jungle.

Who
knows
what kind
of animals
upon
which we'll
stumble?

Checkered Cheetah would love to meet ya...

...after he races and chases Zig Zag Zebra.

Zig Zag Zebra deftly escapes...

...and settles next to Plaid Python, a gigantic snake.

Plaid Python hisses and slithers away...

...past Camouflage Crocodile, who searches for prey.

Camouflage Crocodile dips under water...

...swims 'round Houndstooth Hippo, who couldn't be hotter.

Houndstooth Hippo squats and takes a cool bath...

...then tromps onto shore close to Gingham Giraffe.

Gingham Giraffe stretches high to the sky...

...chews leaves from the trees when Paisley Parrot drops by.

Paisley Parrot dines quickly. Then off she flies...

...over Floral Flamingo and his rock solid thighs.

Floral Flamingo stands watch with his boys...

...spies Argyle Aardvark, who tries not to make noise.

Argyle Aardvark goes and visits his ants...

...by Polka Dot Porcupine performing her happy dance.

Polka Dot Porcupine boogies to her own song...

...while Tie Dye Tortoise inches along.

Tie Dye Tortoise is almost all out of gas...

...when Horizontal Striped Hyena whizzes by fast.

Horizontal Striped Hyena cackles. He's just so delighted...

...as Vertical Striped Vulture circles, and hopes someone will "bite it".

Vertical Striped Vulture is our last patterned friend.

Our jumbled
jungle jaunt
has come to
an end...

...see if you can take what you now know and discover these patterns wherever you go!

Be a Brainy Yak!

Checkered Cheetah

Zig Zag Zebra

Plaid Python

Camouflage Crocodile

Houndstooth Hippo

Gingham Giraffe

Paisley Parrot

Floral Flamingo

Argyle Aardvark

Polka Dot Porcupine

Tie Dye Tortoise

Horizontal Striped Hyena

Vertical Striped Vulture